AVALON
ANTHOLOGY

Copyright © 2023 by Jack Wild Publishing

All rights reserved. No part of this anthology may be reproduced, distributed, or transmitted in any form or by any means, including photocopying, recording, or other electronic or mechanical methods, without the prior written permission of the publisher, except in the case of brief quotations embodied in critical reviews and certain other noncommercial uses permitted by copyright law.

For permission requests, write to the publisher at the following address:

Jack Wild Publishing
508 5TH ST
Marietta, OH 45750
www.jackwildpublishing.com

This anthology is a work of fiction and any resemblance to actual persons, living or dead, or actual events is purely coincidental.

ISBN: 9798864117262

Printed in the United States of America

Cover design by Brittney Arthur

Cover image: Chikovnaya

AVALON ANTHOLOGY

INTRO

Avalon Anthology is a literary oasis where the written word finds its truest expression. It is a place where poets, authors, and creative minds converge to weave human experiences through literature. Our mission is to provide a safe haven for storytellers to share their narratives, explore diverse themes, and touch the hearts of readers worldwide. With each publication, we aim to kindle the fires of imagination, ignite conversations, and leave an indelible mark on the literary landscape.

FALL 2023

Welcome to Avalon Anthology Fall 2023, a lyrical celebration of the beauty, wonder, and inspiration that the natural world has to offer.

This enchanting anthology invites you to immerse yourself in the exquisite verses penned by a diverse array of poets who have found inspiration in the landscapes, creatures, and phenomena that grace our planet.

"Inspirations of the Natural World" is the guiding theme of this collection, uniting the poetic voices within to express the profound connections that bind us to the Earth.

As you turn the pages of this anthology, you will embark on a journey that transcends the boundaries of time and place, venturing into the serene forests, sunlit meadows, and shimmering waters that have long stirred the creative spirits of poets.

EDITOR-IN-CHIEF

BRITTNEY ARTHUR

EDITORS

BRETT GORDON
JAMIE CONWAY

WRITERS

BRETT GORDON
JAMIE CONWAY

POETRY EDITOR

CHRISTOPHER POINDEXTER

Anneleven

CONTRIBUTING WRITERS

SWAPNA SANCHITA
REN MEMETAJ
D. I. HUGHES
KATRYN BROADOAK
CAITLYN LACOVARA
MARIA BEBEN
M. STONEHOUSE
JAMIE CONWAY

KAYLYN MARIE
GUINEVERE JONES
MATTHEW LIEBROSS
W.N.G.
MARIA JEROME
BRETT GORDON
JEN BAGWELL
AURORA RAINE

TO SUBMIT TO FUTURE ANTHOLOGIES, VISIT:
WWW.JACKWILDPUBLISHING.COM/SUBMISSIONS

TABLE OF CONTENTS

Poems

9	"Mountains" by Swapna Sanchita
10	"Earthbound" by Ren Memetaj
11	"Mycelium Mind Mapping" by D. I. Hughes
12	"Appalachia" by Katryn Broadoak
13	"Nature Knows Best" by Caitlyn Lacovara
14	"The Forest" by Maria Beben
15	"Metamorphosis" by M. Stonehouse
16	"Listen to the Trees" by Jamie Conway
18	"Autumn Breeze" by kaylynmarie
19	"Rise Again" by Guinevere Jones
20	"Shaded Garden" by Matthew Liebross
22	"Ethereal Glow" by WNG
23	"Autumn Eyes" by Maria Jerome
24	"Up the Holler" by Brett Gordon
25	"Into the Woods" by Jen Bagwell
26	"Ask Me About the Trees" by Aurora Raine

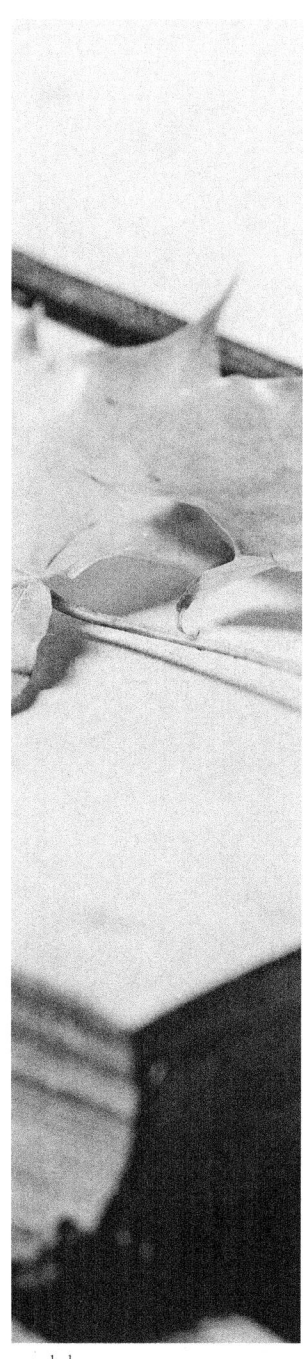

natashabreen

MOUNTAINS
SWAPNA SANCHITA

I wouldn't say I like the mountains
Where walking up their steep inclines
I always find myself bowed down
As if I alone must hold them up
These humungous behemoths that rise
So unnaturally high, touching the skies
Where the air is too rarefied, too clean
And I find myself struggling to breathe
My eyes seeing too much or too little: green
Where even the trees do not look the same
Growing needles instead of ordinary leaves
Too tall, too thin, they bear stones for seeds
The massifs that wear clouds for crowns
Too big, too bold, too stark, too uncertain
The meandering slopes, the wanton winds
The weather and the paths all uncertain
And yet, this is where I meander to
Every time, I desperately need an escape.

EARTHBOUND
REN MEMETAJ

Some people dream of leaving this place, looking for life elsewhere in our universe. Plotting their next steps for colonization of new planets. They dream of some imaginary, undiscovered duplicate earth. Like a new planet is the holy grail that will solve all of humanities problems. But not me. I am earthbound. I am the oceans and the rivers. I am the mountains and the sky. I am all the chemical elements causing the perfect reaction. I belong here. This earth is mine.

MYCELIUM MIND MAPPING
D. I. HUGHES

Burrowed beneath dirt mounds,
we talk in tongues that ground us.
In natural networks, we begin,
unfolding messy as frayed string—
we are the mother

of the earth and all above. I
send forth my fungal waves in
mindful nods to transmit
truth. Only, truth.

We are bigger than The Beatles,
more meandering than the Thames,
as significant as all the people
that have come and gone
before.

We will endure that chaos lurking
in the wind, holding taut yet free.
Thoughts evaporate into roots:
the foundations of forever.

APPALACHIA
KATRYN BROADOAK

Blue Ridges and rolling hills
these are beautiful mountains
though small compared to some

though spectacular to behold
geologically speaking,
the Rockies are only in their teens

these mountains are, in fact, shrinking
sinking back into the earth
whence they were created
hundreds of millions of years ago

appreciate them while they're with us
many generations from now
lifetimes after plates have shifted
children will grow up without them existing

older than Saturn's rings
the caves hidden in these hills
formed long before the dinosaurs
hold mostly rock and stone
they are older than fossils
they are older than bones

NATURE KNOWS BEST
CAITLYN LACOVARA

I want to be Vermont in the fall
Buzzing with color, vibrancy, life
To shed my past with dignity
Even if crowds gather from miles
To watch my hues fade and fall
I want to let go like every leaf
Hanging from the tall beech tree
Burn crimson like maple in October
I want to be free
I want to be.

THE FOREST
MARIA BEBEN

We tasted the ache
like a familiar cocktail,
one we hoped to never drink again.
We took a branch
that posed a danger
and added more kindling,
looking around for anything that would burn.
We gathered and added
until the branch became a forest
and we couldn't see through
to the other side.
We felt betrayed
and confused
and didn't understand how we got there.
We stood on opposite ends of this forest
and felt the weight
of a growing terror.

But at the exact moment
when we reached for a box of matches
to burn it all down,
we remembered that trees have branches
and began to climb.
From the top,
in the clear, crisp air,
we could see
that the forest wasn't a forest at all
just a few trees
that we could help each other
navigate through.
So we climbed back down
and cleared the weeds
and made a path
and together,
celebrated the trees for what they were
before walking out the other side
Together.

METAMORPHOSIS
M. STONEHOUSE

We admired weeping willows that did not weep.
Chased storms that could have drowned us.
We did not flinch or close our eyes.
Standing against the wind with open arms.
We severed the truth from the lies
That were fed to us on recycled plates.
We broke the cages that confined our hearts.
Learned to feed our childhood hungers.
A small voice that learned to sing
Now echoes through an empty cathedral nave.
Light streaming through thick-paned glass
Brings color to a world of gray.
Arthritic hands on instrumental keys
Create a melody in the distance.
How little we notice
Pain and love often exist in the same room.

LISTEN TO THE TREES
JAMIE CONWAY

Trees are alive;
they're growing,
changing,
and feeling,
just like us.

They communicate with each other
deep within the roots;
that's the only way
they know how.

If a smaller, younger tree
needs more sunlight,
the taller trees
slowly part their branches for them.

If there is danger
approaching the system,
they make sure to warn
their neighbours about it.

Why can't we do the same?

Why can't we just
reach deep within
the roots of people
and understand their foundations?

Why can't we just
part our branches
to make sure the sun
does not shine on us alone?

Why can't we just
listen to nature when it speaks?

I'm pretty sure
they've been here
a lot longer than we have.

If we could just learn
a little from the dirt,
perhaps then

the chaos inside us all
would still
just a little.

JAMIE CONWAY

AUTUMN BREEZE
kaylynmarie

The cold
makes me think of you
But somehow
hot weather does too
So many meals
I shared with you
And good times too

When growth takes you
Helps you soar
Fly away
Go on the tour

It might hurt
It might strangle
But give it some time to untangle

You'll find you are where you're meant to be
Changing lives
Even yours, this time

Let yourself breathe
light and love
Through the wounds
Let it shine
As we mend them too
Because it's what you taught us to do

Let the Autumn Breeze carry you

RISE AGAIN
GUINEVERE JONES

One thing is certain
Time goes on and seasons change
Autumn comes and the trees gain their golden crowns
Only to lose them again in the winter
As those gentle giants trade them for a months long slumber
Under plush white blankets
Awoken in the spring
With a vibrant burst of pastel colors

You
My darling
Have a whole forest living inside of you
And like the trees
You will rise again

SHADED GARDEN
MATTHEW LIEBROSS

Wilted.

Amidst a field of wither
A fleeting contrast

You said you'd always cover me
Protect me.
Just remain
Together
In your garden of shade.

Outside your gates
All around, the world grows,
Thrives

Their colors so vibrant
Yet my own refuse to budge.

A step outside your shadows,
the overcast of your heart,
A rejuvenation can be found.

I look up
The sky opens and something within

Spreads

Blossoms

Awakened
Enlightened
Growing once again

How can it be
That my growth
is halted when I'm with you.

Darkness to a flower.

Is it better to bloom
Or *die* within your clouded sky.

MATTHEW LIEBROSS

ETHEREAL GLOW

My eye is never idle to capture
Nature's ethereal glow
As the sun sets, with its
Fiery beauty, juxtaposed
With win, the birds follow
its flow.

WNG

AUTUMN EYES
MARIA JEROME

Autumn eyes gazing back at me.
A swirl of colors like a forest I can get lost in.
Brown bark and Dewey moss, sun kissed with blazing amber.
You chill me to the bone like a cool harvest wind and although mesmerizing,
They haunt me for we all know autumn is an ending;
but a beautiful one at that

UP THE HOLLER
BRETT GORDON

there's a little A-frame
cabin and in autumn, Owl
perks up because he knows its
his time to shine- *Athene Noctua*.
He perches close. When the
wind rustles neon leaves, he tells
of their lives passed as they
litter and dance on the breeze.
He's the watcher, the
keeper, the storyteller.

The cast iron kettle is calling now-
a promise of warm soul
satisfaction. By the fire we
listen to Owl. He soothsays:
*prepare yourselves for a
vengeful winter, doubly stack
your wood. Dawn will be
buried under the heavy weight
of night two months longer
than usual.*

INTO THE WOODS
JEN BAGWELL

A break in the trees allows the moonlight to spill over me
As I sit stoically under this old elm
I inhale deeply
My mind is a treacherous, and this is the only place I feel a sense of belonging
This certainty
This is what the entirety of my existence has felt like
Solitary
Left to find my own way through the darkness
Learning to embrace the rush of adrenaline when a twig snaps
There are so many things that could inflict pain here
But they don't
Not like the others do in the light
The monsters inside of these evergreen walls seem to be satisfied in allowing me to exist
unscathed
I think they know I'm not able to exist anywhere else
This is the only place I ever want to return to
The only place that welcomes me like an old friend

ASK ME ABOUT THE TREES
AURORA RAINE

Ask me about the trees-
And I will tell you how their arms carried me.
How I found heaven glistening through the branches of a giant oak.
I will tell you about the bird who gave me sticks to build a new nest when I had lost my own.
How the wounds grew wildflowers.
How the wildflowers became a crown over me
and I sprouted pine tree branch wings.
Do you hear the birds singing in fives and threes.
Stick this fern feather in your hat
and dance with me to the beat of the wood peckers drum.
All I have ever wanted is to watch the rain
and see petals falling from cherry blossom trees.
Ask me about the trees.

Printed in Great Britain
by Amazon